Fenimore's Gift To Santa

There's a special place
called Berry Town, where
joy fills the air.

All the children were
excited when Santa came
last year.

He brought gifts for all the children, but now there's sadness in the air!

There were letters mailed to each house in Berry Town.

Fenimore's mother read her letter.

4

The letter said,
"Dear Fenimore,
I know you've been good
this year.
I am very sick! I won't
be able to bring you gifts.
Cheer up Fenimore, there
will be plenty more
Christmas for sure.

Love, Santa!"

"Dear Fenimore,
I know you've been good this year.
I am very sick! I won't be able to bring you gifts.
Cheer up Fenimore, there
will be plenty more Christmas for sure.

Love, Santa!

Fenimore became very sad.

"Mom, that's not fair. Why did Santa get sick this year?" "Fenimore, do you remember when you got sick? You needed days of rest. Now it's Santa's turn to get better."

"Mom! I understand." Fenimore had a plan!

Thank you mom

He went for the phone and he called the North Pole. Elf Bernard picked up the phone!

"Hello, Fenimore!"

"Hi, I'm worried about Santa," Said Fenimore.

"Santa really wanted to visit Berry Town. You'll see Santa next year! Rodolph and all the reindeers are by his side." Elf Bernard replied.

"I'm glad," Said Fenimore.

Hi Fenimore
NORTH POLE

"Mrs. Claus made Santa her special soup! Filled with the North Pole's Jollaloo!"

"Ha! Ha!" Fenimore laughed. "Well, please tell Santa that I called."

"I will," Said Elf Bernard.

Z
Z
Z
Jollaloo soup
14

Fenimore felt better, but he wanted to do more for Santa!

Fenimore went into his room. He wanted to make his idea come true.

He took up his piggy bank and shook out his money he got from Uncle Frank.

Then he went into the living room to talk to his mom.

Mom, I have an amazing idea!
Let's send a gift to Santa.
Poor guy travels far.
He must have made a "million trips,
and now it made him very sick!"

"I think that's a great idea.
His mom replied.

Let me help you order this gift online.
I'll use my BERRY CARD Fenimore.
"Thank you mom!"

1 million trips
18

Fenimore looked online with
his mom.
Then he saw a red sweater.
"That's the one, Mom!"

Fenimore's Mom ordered the
red sweater.

"Thanks Mom."
Then Fenimore went to bed.

Berry Town online store
$7
20

Fenimore's mom thought of
a great idea. She then send a
message to all the parents
in Berry Town.

The message read,

"Hello parents, let's all help Santa.
We can buy our children
lots of gifts."

All the parents agreed.

Hello parents,
let's all help
Santa.We can
buy our children
lots of
gifts.

All the children in Berry Town were fast asleep. So their parents bought their children's gifts and snuck it under their trees.

It was finally Christmas
and all the children woke up
to see their gifts.
All the parents in Berry
Town made
their children happy.

MERRY CHRISTMAS
26

Fenimore woke up and
jumped out of bed. He
then went into the living room.

"Merry Christmas Fenimore!
I love you!" Said his Mom.

Fenimore's Mom handed him
a gift. Fenimore couldn't
believe his eyes.

"Oh wow Mom, I love you,
you're just like Santa!"

"I love you too" His Mom
replied.

Christmas

The phone rang. It was Santa calling from the North Pole.

"Ho! Ho! Ho! Thank you Fenimore, for being so kind. I love my new sweater. I'm feeling much better! Christmas is about being kind," Said Santa.

"I'm glad you like it," Fenimore replied.

Then Santa Picked up his Christmas Bell. "Ho! Ho! Ho! Merry Christmas everyone! Thank you Parents, you've all done a great job." Everyone in Berry Town could hear Santa from inside their house. "This is the best Christmas I've ever had." Said Fenimore.

And so ever since that day,
the parents in Berry
Town helped Santa
whenever he's not feeling well!

The End!

Merry Christmas
"Thank you mom."
36

Fenimore's gift to Santa.

This is a fictional storyline. However, it's an amazing Christmas story.

Berry Town is a fictional town that Santa visits every Christmas. Santa is not feeling well and won't be able to deliver gifts for the children. Santa sent letters telling everyone that he won't be able to deliver the presents. Fenimore, the main character in the story, isn't happy. His mother encouraged him not to worry. Fenimore is a kind little boy, and he wanted to make Santa feel better. He thought of a great idea to make Santa feel special.

In the real world, we all like to feel special. I also wanted to show that sometimes giving can be rewarding. I enjoyed writing this storyline. I hope your little ones love this book. Thank you.

My name is Ashia Foster. I'm the author of this wonderful
Christmas story. This will be my fifth children's book.
I'm a new author, and I'm really enjoying writing stories
for children. In all my books, your children will certainly
be entertained. There's also something, one can take
from my stories, a positive message, including joy.

You can also find my other books on Amazon.com. There's
the eBook version for these books on Amazon Kindle

Away from my friends because of Corona
The Park Is Open Inside
Allman Town Changed With Sam's Mother"s Cake
Lets Read And Play With Pinkaline

Thanks for all your support in purchasing my books.